THE PIÑATA

THAT THE FARM MAIDEN HUNG

SAMANTHA R. VAMOS

ILLUSTRATED BY SEBASTIÀ SERRA

iᴍi Charlesbridge

For Randa Wright and Valerie Vlahos with love.
And for Greg and Jackson, who have always believed.—S. R. V.

To Marta and Sira with love.—S. S.

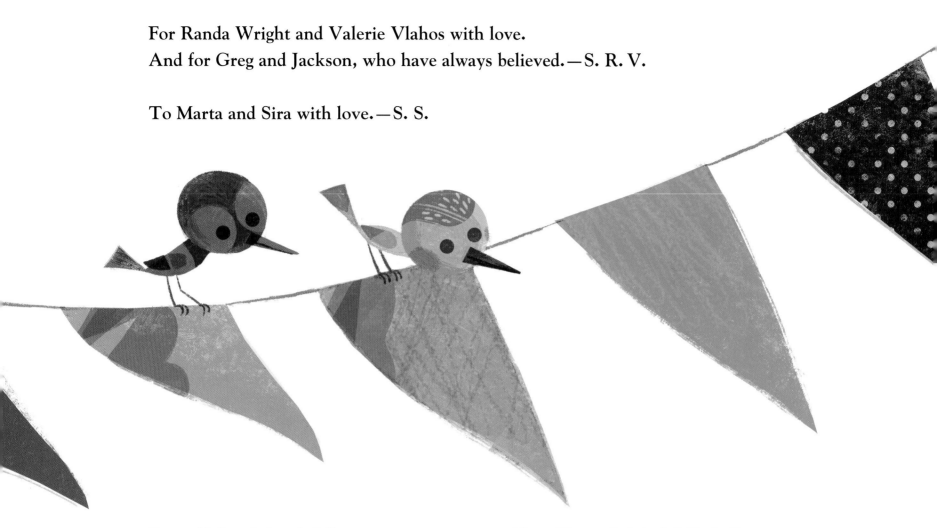

Text copyright © 2019 by Samantha R. Vamos
Illustrations copyright © 2019 by Sebastià Serra
All rights reserved, including the right of reproduction in whole
or in part in any form. Charlesbridge and colophon are registered
trademarks of Charlesbridge Publishing, Inc.

Published by Charlesbridge
85 Main Street
Watertown, MA 02472
(617) 926-0329
www.charlesbridge.com

Printed in China
(hc) 10 9 8 7 6 5 4 3 2

Illustrations made with Photoshop and other software and
    colored pencil
Display type and text type set in Posada and Goudy
Color separations by Colourscan Print Co Pte Ltd. in Singapore
Printed by 1010 Printing International Limited in Huizhou,
    Guangdong, China
Production supervision by Brian G. Walker
Designed by Susan Mallory Sherman

Library of Congress Cataloging-in-Publication Data
Names: Vamos, Samantha R., author. | Serra, Sebastià, 1966–
    illustrator.
Title: The piñata that the farm maiden hung / Samantha R. Vamos;
    illustrated by Sebastià Serra.
Description: Watertown, MA: Charlesbridge, [2019] | Text in
    English, with Spanish words. | Summary: Using the building
    verse of "The House that Jack Built," a farm girl creates a
    piñata of papier-mâché with the help of a boy and the animals
    on the farm. Includes a glossary of Spanish words, and a step-
    by-step guide to building your own piñata.
Identifiers: LCCN 2017055935 | ISBN 9781580897969 (reinforced
    for library use) | ISBN 9781632896247 (ebook pdf)
    | ISBN 9781632896230 (e-book)
Subjects: LCSH: Nursery rhymes. | Piñatas—Juvenile fiction. |
    Farm life—Juvenile fiction. | Domestic animals—Juvenile
    fiction. | Stories in rhyme. | CYAC: Stories in rhyme. |
    Piñatas—Fiction. | Farm life—Fiction. | Domestic animals—
    Fiction. | LCGFT: Nursery rhymes.
Classification: LCC PZ8.3.V32537 Pi 2019 | DDC 398.8 [E]—dc23
    LC record available at https://lccn.loc.gov/2017055935

THIS IS THE PIÑATA that the farm maiden hung.

This is the boy
who shaped the clay
to make the **PIÑATA**
that the farm maiden hung.

This is the horse
that hauled the water
and carried the **NIÑO**
who shaped the **BARRO**
to make the **PIÑATA**
that the farm maiden hung.

This is the goose
that stirred a paste
with flour and **AGUA**
hauled by the **CABALLO**
that carried the **NIÑO**
who shaped the **BARRO**
to make the **PIÑATA** that the farm maiden hung.

This is the cat
that tore the paper
to soak in the **PASTA**
stirred by the **GANSO**
with flour and **AGUA**
hauled by the **CABALLO**
that carried the **NIÑO**
who shaped the **BARRO**
to make the **PIÑATA**
   that the farm maiden hung.

This is the sheep
that braided a rope
then wrapped the **PAPEL**
torn by the **GATO**
and soaked in the **PASTA**
stirred by the **GANSO**
with flour and **AGUA**
hauled by the **CABALLO**
that carried the **NIÑO**
who shaped the **BARRO**
to make the **PIÑATA** that the farm maiden hung.

This is the farmer
who carved figures from wood
while minding the **OVEJA**
that braided the **CUERDA**
then wrapped the **PAPEL**
torn by the **GATO**
and soaked in the **PASTA**
stirred by the **GANSO**
with flour and **AGUA**
hauled by the **CABALLO**
that carried the **NIÑO**
who shaped the **BARRO**
to make the **PIÑATA** that the farm maiden hung.

As the warm sun dried the **PIÑATA**,
the **GANSO** poured confetti into painted eggshells,
the **CABALLO** picked clusters of brilliant bluebells,

the **NIÑO** trimmed a banner of tissue-paper flags,
the **OVEJA** and **GATO** raced in burlap-sack bags,
the **CAMPESINO** carved more **ALEBRIJES**—a fox, frog, and bat—
and the farm maiden baked a cake in the shape of a hat.

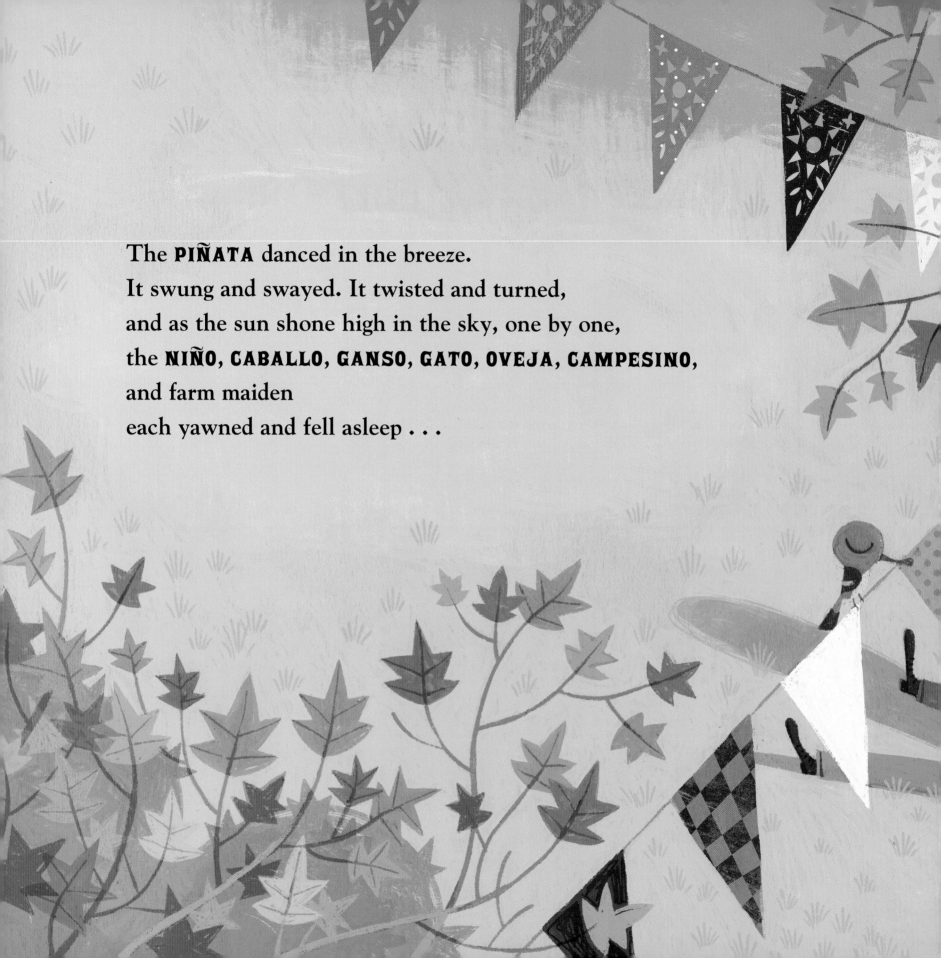

The **PIÑATA** danced in the breeze.
It swung and swayed. It twisted and turned,
and as the sun shone high in the sky, one by one,
the **NIÑO, CABALLO, GANSO, GATO, OVEJA, CAMPESINO,**
and farm maiden
each yawned and fell asleep . . .

. . . and no one filled the **PIÑATA** that the farm maiden hung.

Just as the moon began to rise, the farm maiden stirred and cried, "Ay!" waking the **NIÑO**, **CABALLO**, **GANSO**, **GATO**, **OVEJA**, and **CAMPESINO**, and together they hurried to fill, seal, and decorate the **PIÑATA**.

When the **PIÑATA** was finally ready, everyone yelled, "**¡SORPRESA!**" and "**¡FELIZ CUMPLEAÑOS!**" to the birthday girl . . .

. . . who hit the **PIÑATA** that the **CAMPESINA** hung.

La Canción de la Piñata

Dale, dale, dale.
No pierdas el tino.
Porque si lo pierdes,
pierdes el camino.
Ya le diste una,
ya le diste dos,
ya le diste tres,
y tu tiempo se acabó!

The Piñata Song

Hit it, hit it, hit it.
Don't lose your aim.
Because if you lose it,
you will lose your way.
You hit it one,
you hit it two,
you hit it three times,
and your time is up!

MAKE YOUR OWN PIÑATA!

A *piñata* is a container created by covering a balloon or clay pot with strips of paper soaked in a glue-like paste. The *piñata* is decorated with paint and/or tissue paper and typically filled with candy and toys. It is hung, from a tree or pole, for example, and people try to hit it with a wooden dowel or broomstick to break it open.

MATERIALS

balloon (12-inch latex)

newspaper

scissors

water (1 cup)

large bowl

all-purpose white flour (1¼ cup)

whisk

rope or twine (36 inches or longer)

wrapped candy, small toys, and/or other novelty
  items

duct tape

colored tissue paper, cut into squares

paint, brushes, and craft glue

optional: a small fan

INSTRUCTIONS

This project, including drying time, takes a few days. Before you begin, read all the instructions so you can plan ahead, and be sure to ask an adult for permission and help because making a *piñata* can be messy. You may want to wear an apron or old shirt and cover your work area to protect against spills.

1. BLOW UP the balloon and tie it with a knot.

2. CUT the newspaper into strips (approximately 1½ to 2 inches wide by 6 inches long). Cut enough strips to cover your balloon with two layers.

3. ADD THE WATER to the bowl. Gradually add small amounts of flour, using the whisk to mix until very few lumps remain and the consistency is like a white glue. If the paste is too thick or too thin, add a little more water or flour to balance it out.

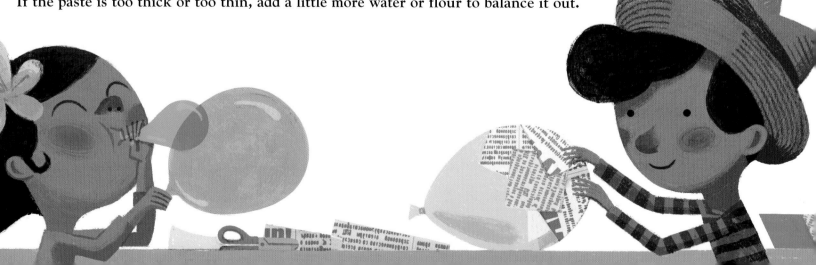

4. DIP a newspaper strip into the paste, coating the strip on both sides. Use your fingers to skim off any excess paste from each side of the strip.

5. APPLY the coated strip—either vertically or horizontally—to the balloon, gently smoothing the strip across the balloon with your fingers.

6. REPEAT STEPS 4 AND 5 until the balloon is covered. All the strips should be applied in the same direction. Make sure not to cover the balloon's knot so you can remove it later from inside your *piñata*.

7. THROW OUT any remaining paste. Let the strips dry for eight to twelve hours. To shorten the drying time, you can use a fan to blow on the balloon. The strips will create a hardened shell over the balloon.

8. After the balloon has dried, **MAKE** a second batch of paste and repeat steps 4 and 5 to apply a second layer of strips. If the first layer was applied horizontally, apply the second layer vertically and vice versa.

9. FOLD your rope or twine in half and place the middle point at the opposite end of the balloon from where it is tied. Paste a strip over the middle point, adding more strips to secure the rope or twine to the balloon.

10. Let the balloon sit for two or three days to **DRY** completely. If desired, use your fan again.

11. Once your *piñata* is totally dry, use your scissors to **POP** the balloon where the knot is tied. Gently pull the popped balloon out. Now you have a small hole to insert treats. If the hole is too small, enlarge it a little by cutting around the edge to make a slightly larger circle.

12. FILL the *piñata* with candy, small toys, and/or other items.

13. YOU CAN COVER the hole with strips of paper coated in a new batch of paste, or you can simply cover it securely with a few pieces of duct tape to be sure nothing will fall out.

14. DECORATE the *piñata* using paint and by gluing tissue-paper squares to cover it.

DEFINITIONS

ALEBRIJES (ah-ley-BREE-heys) are wooden animal and imaginary-creature figurines that are hand-painted with vibrant colors. They are Oaxacan-Mexican folk art and were originally made in the 1930s by artist Pedro Linares López out of papier-mâché.

CASCARONES (cas-cah-RO-nays) are drained and dried eggshells that are decorated and filled with confetti. They are popular at celebrations including birthdays, weddings, and holidays. A *cascarón* broken over one's head is supposed to be good luck.

PAPEL PICADO (pah-PEL peh-CAH-doh) is a traditional Mexican art form in which small flags or panels made of tissue paper are cut into intricate designs and/or words. *Papel picado* is often displayed for birthdays, weddings, funerals, holidays, and religious celebrations.

GLOSSARY OF SPANISH WORDS

AGUA (AH-gwah): water

BARRO (BAR-roh): clay

CABALLO (ka-BAH-yoh): horse

CAMPESINA (kam-peh-SEEN-ah): farm maiden

CAMPESINO (kam-peh-SEEN-oh): farmer

CUERDA (KWER-dah): rope

¡FELIZ CUMPLEAÑOS! (fe-LIS koom-pley-AN-yos): Happy Birthday!

GANSO (GAN-soh): goose

GATO (GAH-toh): cat

NIÑO (NEEN-yo): a boy child

OVEJA (oh-BEY-hah): sheep

PAPEL (pah-PEL): paper

PASTA (PAHS-tah): paste

SORPRESA (sor-PRAY-sah): surprise